MW00885589

What
Pandas
do when no one's looking
(and other nonsense)

What pandas do when no one's looking (and other nonsense)

Written and illustrated by K. J. Hobart

Published by Padweasel
www.padweasel.com

All rights reserved. Subject to statutory exceptions and to provisions of relevant collective licensing agreements, no part of this publication may be reproduced without prior written permission of the author.

The moral right of Karen J. Hobart to be identified as the author and illustrator of this book has been asserted in accordance with the Copyright, Designs and Patents Act 1988.

ISBN 978-1-8380359-5-2

padweasel

A panda will tell you that they love bamboo.
But there is a secret they're keeping from you.
When they're alone and there's no one to see...

they love nothing more than a nice cup of tea!

The lion will tell you that he loves to hunt.
A tasty gazelle may well take the brunt.
But when he's alone and there's no one to look...

he'd rather relax with his head in a book!

It's thought that flamingos like to stand on one leg.
Like they're fixed to the ground with a long skinny peg.
But when they're at home and there's no one to see...

they sit with their feet up and watch loads of TV!

Giraffe spends all day munching down lots of leaves,
(so the casual onlooker naively believes).
But what you can't see when you look from afar...

is her driving around in a red racing car!

We all think we know how zebras behave.
They travel in herds, in a big stripy wave.
But when no one's looking they'll act on a whim...

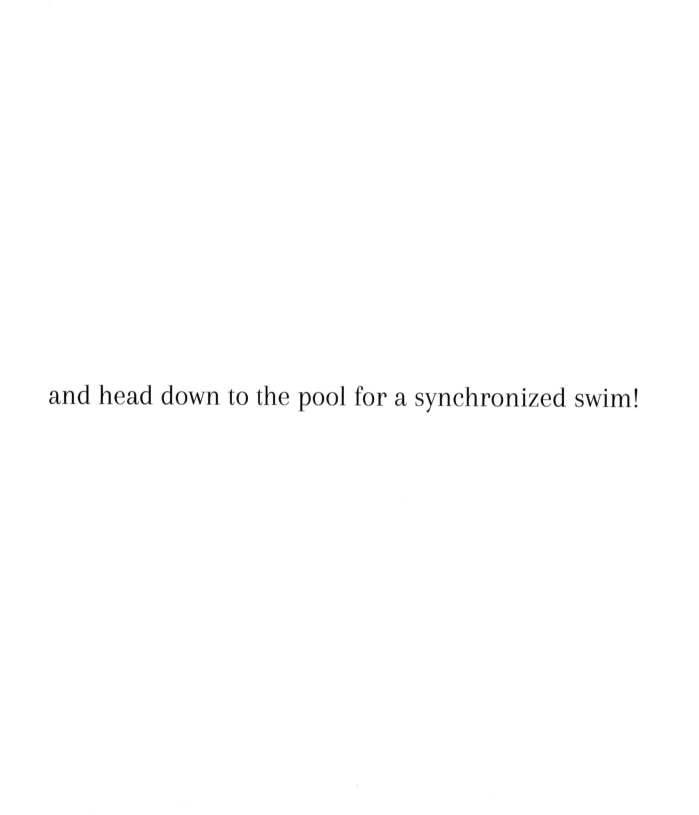

and head down to the pool for a synchronized swim!

Everyone knows what sharks get up to.
Swimming around with a do do do doo.
But what they like best when they're all by themselves...

is to build flat pack cupboards and
put up some shelves!

Is there a thing that you like to do,
when no one's around and it's just you?

(Or when you're all alone and anything goes,
do you sit in your undies and just pick your nose?!)

invent a game with hundreds of rules!

impersonate dinosaurs!

design a spaceship!

read about jelly fish!

sing a cheesy pop song!

write a poem about magical woodlice!

contemplate your belly button!

dance!

draw aliens!

build a den!

name your toes!

padweasel

Printed in Great Britain
by Amazon

47217660R00017